Brave as a Mountain Lion

by Ann Herbert Scott
Illustrated by Glo Coalson

HOUGHTON MIFFLIN

Boston • Atlanta • Dallas • Geneva, Illinois • Palo Alto • Princeton

For Arthur Badugwiche Dick
and for all his family
–A.H.S.

For my father, Bill
–G.C.

Clarion Books
a Houghton Mifflin Company imprint
215 Park Avenue South, New York, NY 10003
Text copyright © 1996 by Ann Herbert Scott
Illustrations copyright © 1996 by Glo Coalson

The illustrations for this book were executed in watercolor
and pastel on Arches 90-lb. watercolor paper.
The text was set in 14/17-point Garamond.

For information about this and other Houghton Mifflin trade and reference books and
multimedia products, visit The Bookstore at Houghton Mifflin on the World Wide Web at
(http://www.hmco.com/trade/).
Printed in the U.S.A.

Library of Congress Cataloging-in-Publication Data
Scott, Ann Herbert.
Brave as a mountain lion / by Ann Herbert Scott ; illustrated by Glo Coalson.
p.   cm.
Summary: Spider is afraid to get up on stage in front of everybody in the school
spelling bee, but after listening to his father's advice, decides that he too will try
to be as brave as his Shoshoni ancestors.
ISBN 0-395-66760-7
[1. Courage—Fiction. 2. Stage fright—Fiction. 3. Schools—Fiction.
4. Shoshoni Indians—Fiction. 5. Indians of North America—Fiction.]
I. Coalson, Glo, ill.   II. Title.
PZ7.S415Bt   1996
[Fic]—dc20   94-42906
                                                    CIP
                                                    AC

3456789-WC-04 03 02 01 00 99 98

It was snowing hard. Pressing his face against the cold glass of the living room window, Spider could barely see his father's horses crowding against the fence. Soon the reservation would be covered with darkness.

Spider shivered. Any other night he would have been hoping his father would reach home before the snow drifted too high to push through. But tonight was different. Tonight he dreaded his father's coming.

In his pocket Spider could feel two pieces of paper from school. One he wanted to show his father. One he didn't. Not tonight. Not ever.

Beside him on the couch his sister Winona was playing with her doll. Lucky kid, thought Spider. Winona was too little to worry about anything, especially school.

Just then Spider saw the blinking red lights of the snowplow
clearing the road beside their house. Right behind came his father's
new blue pickup. Spider sighed. At least Dad was home safe. Now
the trouble would begin!

Winona ran to the back door. But Spider stayed on the couch, waiting. From the kitchen he could smell dinner cooking. His favorite, deer meat. But tonight he didn't even feel like eating. Soon he heard the sound of his father and his brother Will stomping the snow from their boots.

Spider's father came in with an armful of mail from the post office. He hung up his hat and jacket on the pegs by the kitchen and stretched out in his favorite chair.

"So what did you do in school today?" he asked Spider.

"Not much," said Spider, feeling his pocket.

"Did you bring home any papers?"

Spider nodded. How did his father always know?

"Let's take a look," said his father.

Spider took the first paper from his pocket. "Here's the good one," he said.

"Spelling one hundred percent. Every word correct. Good for you, son."

"But, Dad, I'm in trouble." Spider shoved the other paper into his father's hand. "The teacher wants me to be in the big school spelling bee."

Spider's father read out loud: "Dear Parent, I am pleased to inform you that your son Spider has qualified for the school spelling bee, which will be held next Thursday night. We hope you and your family will attend."

Spider's mother and grandmother came in from the kitchen with the platter of deer meat and bowls of beans and corn for dinner. "That's a good report, Little Brother," his grandmother said, smiling.

"But I won't do it," said Spider.

"Why not?" asked Will.

"I'm too afraid," said Spider.

"But you're a brave boy," said his father. "Why are you afraid?"

"Dad," said Spider, "you have to stand high up on the stage in the gym and all the people look at you. I'm afraid my legs would freeze together and I wouldn't be able to walk. And if I did get up there, no sound would come out when I opened my mouth. It's too scary."

"Oh, I see," said his father.

Spider's mother put her hand on his shoulder. "You must be hungry. Let's eat."

———————

After dinner Spider sat by the wood stove doing his homework. "Dad, were you ever in a spelling bee?" he asked.

"As a matter of fact, I was."

"Were you scared?"

"I was very scared. I didn't even want to do it. But then my father told me to pretend I was a brave animal, the strongest, bravest animal I could think of. Then I wasn't afraid anymore."

Later, Spider sat up in bed thinking of animals who weren't afraid of anything. Above his head hung the picture of a mountain lion his dad had painted for him. How about a mountain lion, the King of the Beasts?

Spider took his flashlight from under his pillow and shined its beam on the face of the great wild creature. "Brave as a mountain lion," he said to himself in a loud, strong voice.

"Brave as a mountain lion," he repeated in his mind as he was falling asleep.

"I'll try to be brave as a mountain lion," he whispered to his father the next morning as he brushed his hair for school.

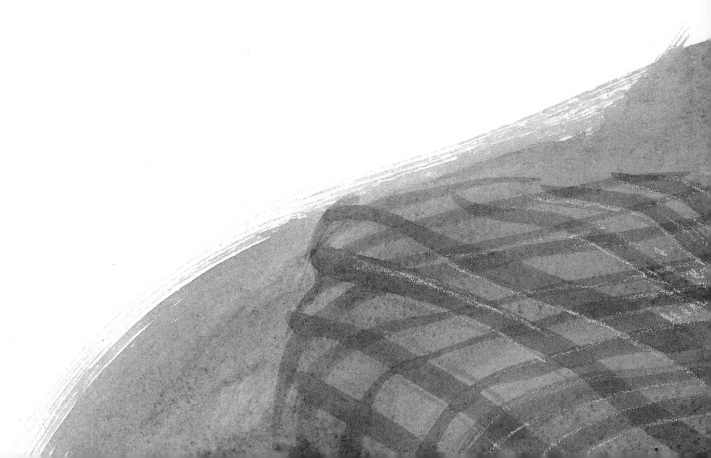

At recess the next day Spider peeked into the gymnasium. The huge room was empty. He looked up at the mural painting of the western Shoshone people of long ago. They were brave hunters of deer and antelope and elk, just as his father and his uncles were today.

At the far end of the gym was the scoreboard with the school's emblem, the eagle. Every Saturday in the winter Spider and his whole family came to cheer for Will and the basketball team. Those players weren't afraid of anything.

Then Spider stared up at the stage. That's where the spellers would stand. He could feel his throat tighten and hear his heart thumping, bumpity-bumpity-bumpity-bump. How could he ever get up there in front of all the people? Spider ran outside, slamming the gym door behind him.

That afternoon it was still snowing. At home Spider found his grandmother beading a hatband for his father's birthday. Spider watched her dip her needle into the bowls of red and black and white beads.

"Grandma, were you ever in a spelling bee?"

"No, I never was," his grandmother answered. "Are you thinking much about it?"

"All the time," said Spider.

"What's the worst part?"

"Being up on the stage with all the people looking at you."

"Oh, that's easy," said his grandmother. "You can be clever. Clever as a coyote. The coyote always has some trick to help him out of trouble. When you're up there on the stage, you don't have to look at the people. You can turn your back on them and pretend they aren't even there."

In bed that night Spider pulled the covers over his head. "Brave as a mountain lion, clever as a coyote," he kept repeating to himself as he fell asleep.

The next morning Spider scraped a peephole in the ice on his bedroom window. He couldn't see the far mountains for the swirling snow. He smiled as he packed his book bag. If it kept snowing like this, maybe the principal would close school tomorrow.

In class that day all everybody could talk about was the spelling bee. "Can we count on you, Spider?" asked Miss Phillips, his teacher.

Spider shook his head. "Maybe," he said. "I haven't made up my mind."

"You'd better make up your mind soon," said Miss Phillips. "The spelling bee is tomorrow night."

After lunch Spider walked by the gym door, but this time he didn't open it. He didn't have to. He remembered just how everything looked. Scary. When he thought about it, a shiver went all the way down his spine.

By the afternoon the snow had piled in drifts higher than Spider's head. Spider got a bowl of popcorn and went to the carport to watch Will shoot baskets. Time after time the ball slipped through the net. Will almost never missed.

"How about some popcorn for me?" Will asked his little brother. Spider brought back another bowl from the kitchen.

"Are you practicing for the spelling bee?" asked Will.

"I've decided not to be in it," said Spider. "I'm going to be brave when I'm bigger."

Will nodded. "I remember those spelling bees."

"Were you afraid?" asked Spider.

"I was scared silly," said Will. "I was so scared I was afraid I'd wet my pants. Then I learned the secret."

"What's the secret?" asked Spider.

"To be silent."

"Silent?" asked Spider. "What does that do?"

"It keeps you cool. When I have a hard shot to make and the whole team depends on me, that's when I get very silent."

Spider didn't say anything. He just watched his brother shooting one basket after another. Then he saw her. High above the shelves of paint and livestock medicines was a tiny insect. It was his old friend, Little Spider, dangling on a long strand as she spun a new part of her web. She was silent. Silent as the moon.

Spider laughed. How could he have forgotten! Grandmother often told him how when he was a baby in his cradle board he used to watch for hours while a little spider spun her web above his head. She had been his first friend. Ever since, his family had called him Spider.

Taking the stepladder, Spider climbed up close so he could watch the tiny creature. How brave she was, dropping down into space with nothing to hang onto. And how clever, weaving a web out of nothing but her own secret self. "Say something," he whispered.

The little insect was silent. But Spider felt she was talking to him in her own mysterious way. "Listen to your spirit," she seemed to say. "Listen to your spirit and you'll never be afraid."

The next morning the snow had stopped. Outside Spider's window icicles glistened in the sun. No chance of school being closed today.

"Brave as a mountain lion, clever as a coyote, silent as a spider," Spider thought to himself as he buttoned his vest.

Winona pushed open the door. "Are you going to do it?"

"I'm going to do it," Spider answered.

That night all the family came, his grandmother who lived with them and his other grandparents and his father and his mother and three aunts and two uncles and Will and Winona and lots of their cousins. Three of his cousins were going to be in the spelling bee, too.

Brave as a mountain lion, Spider climbed up the steps to the stage. Clever as a coyote, he turned his back so he wouldn't see the rows of people down below. Silently, he listened to his spirit. Bumpity-bump-bump went his heart.

All the best spellers in his class were up there on the stage, standing in a line. The principal gave them the words, one by one.

At first the words were easy. "Yellow," said the principal. "I have a yellow dog."

Spider kept his eyes on the principal's face. "Yellow," said Spider. "Y-e-l-l-o-w. Yellow."

"Correct," said the principal.

Then the words got a little harder. "February," said the principal. "Soon it will be February." It was Spider's turn again.

"February," said Spider, remembering the *r*. "Capital f-e-b-r-u-a-r-y. February."

"Correct," said the principal.

Finally there were only two spellers left standing—Spider and Elsie, a girl from the other side of the reservation.

"Terrific," said the principal. "We have a terrific basketball team."

"Terrific," said Spider, taking a big breath. "T-e-r-r-i-f-f-i-c. Terrific."

"Incorrect," said the principal. Then he turned to Elsie. "Terrific. We have a terrific basketball team."

"Terrific," said Elsie. "T-e-r-r-i-f-i-c. Terrific."

"Correct," said the principal. "Let's give a hand to our two winners from Miss Phillips' class: Elsie in first place and Spider in second place."

It was over! Spider climbed down the steps and found the rows where his family were sitting. Spider's father shook his hand and Will slapped him on the back. "You did it!" his mother said proudly. "You stood right up there in front of everybody!"

"It was easy," said Spider.

"You were brave," said his father. "Brave as a mountain lion."

"And clever," said his grandmother. "Clever as a coyote."

I wasn't even afraid, Spider thought. I listened to my spirit. "But now I'm hungry," he told his family. "Hungry as a bear. Let's all go home and eat."

"My story has its roots in the beautiful Western Shoshone country of northeastern Nevada," says **Ann Herbert Scott**. "Over a period of years I have visited that high ranching country whenever I can, often staying with friends on the Owyhee Reservation. The story idea came directly from a boy who was confronted by an everyday challenge to his courage: his fear of standing up before an audience as part of the annual school spelling bee."

Ann Herbert Scott is the author of several books for Clarion: *Someday Rider, Grandmother's Chair, On Mother's Lap, A Brand Is Forever,* and *Cowboy Country.* She lives in Santa Rosa, California.

Glo Coalson previously collaborated with Ann Herbert Scott on *On Mother's Lap.* For *Brave As a Mountain Lion,* Ms. Coalson traveled to Nevada to spend time with Owyhee children both in and out of school. Raised in Abilene, she now lives in Garland, Texas.